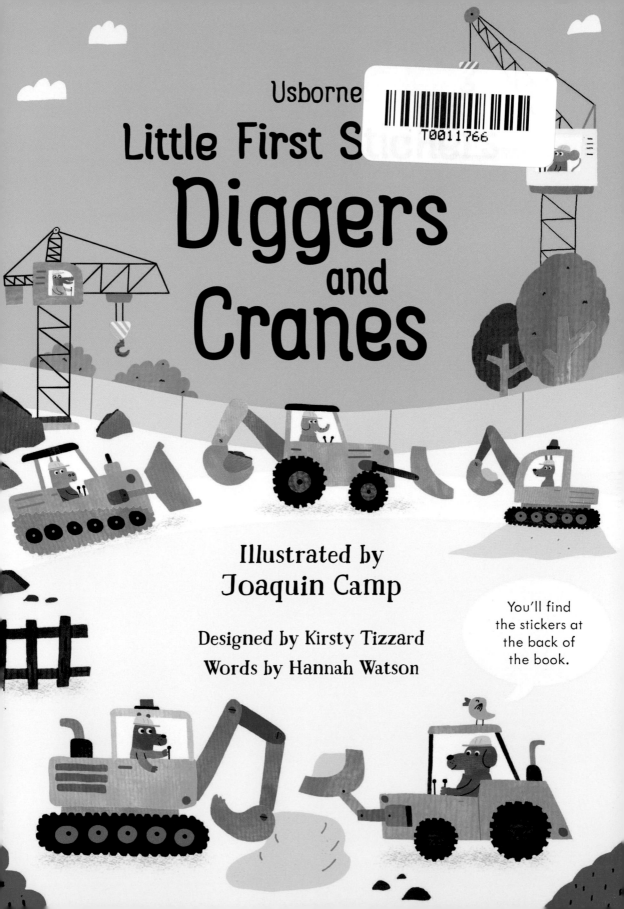

Usborne
Little First Stickers
Diggers
and
Cranes

Illustrated by
Joaquin Camp

Designed by Kirsty Tizzard
Words by Hannah Watson

You'll find
the stickers at
the back of
the book.

Lifting and loading

In this scrapyard, cranes sort old cars so their parts can be used again. Stick on some cranes lifting cars and collecting metal.

Find a crane to pick up this old car.

Add a magnet crane collecting metal.

Stick on a dog
carrying car tyres.

3

Carrying cargo

At the port, big cranes are used to load cargo on to ships. Add lots of busy workers moving crates of fruit.

Stick some cranes
on the ship's deck.

Fill this road with trucks.

Snowdrift

Diggers must come to the rescue to clear
the snow blocking this road. Find a tow truck
to pull the blue car out of a snowdrift, too.

Stick on a crane collecting logs.

Add a digger tipping snow into this truck.

Find a big crane to help move this tree.

7

Building higher

Cranes are needed to complete these new buildings. They will be the tallest in the town. Finish the picture with stickers.

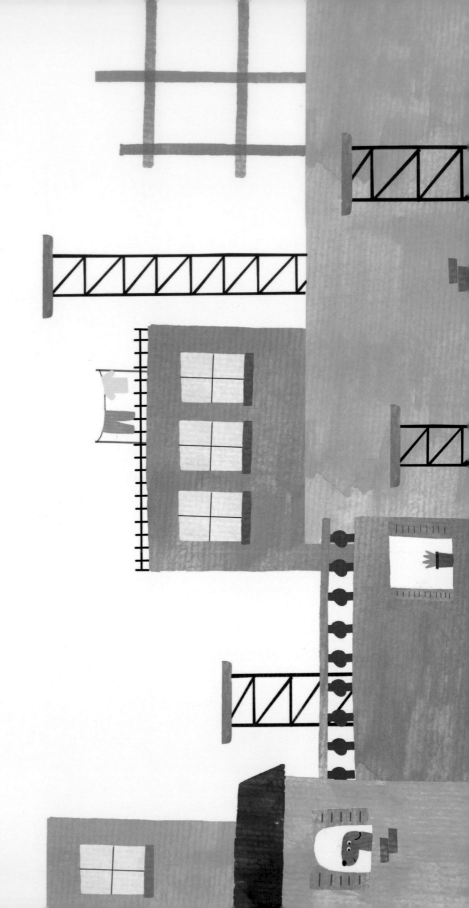

Stick a crane lifting bricks on this rooftop.

Find a window for this crane to lift.

9

Roadworks

The water pipes under the road need to be fixed. Add diggers to clear away the soil, and a crane to lift new pipes into place.

Find a plumber to help fix this burst pipe.

WC

BOOKS

Find a crane to lift these pipes.

Create a traffic jam along this road.

In a quarry

Diggers scoop out heavy pieces of rock from
the quarry. They will be used to make buildings.
Add lots of diggers trundling up this track.

SLOW

Demolition

Cranes, diggers and other big machines are needed to pull down old buildings so new ones can be built.

Max capacity 2 animals

Stick on some animals overseeing the site.

Find lots of cranes to demolish this building.

KEEP CLEAR

Find a tractor to *pull* this cart to safety.

Playground

Add lots of machines to this picture
to help build a playground.

Find a crane lifting a roundabout.

Add a digger
filling a sandpit.

Lifting and loading

Snowdrift

Building higher pages 8-9

Roadworks pages 10-11

In a quarry pages 12-13

SLOW

Demolition pages 14-15

CAUTION

Playground page 16

You could put these stickers anywhere in the book.

SLOW

CAUTION